ALFIE

(The turtle that disappeared)

THYRA HEDER

Abrams Books for Young Readers

New York

On my sixth birthday, I got Alfie.

The lady at the store said he looked about six too.
We were six, together.

At home, on my carpet, he stood very still.

I introduced him to everyone.

I taught him my wiggle dance and made him presents,
but he didn't seem to notice.

I showed him my costumes and wrote him songs.
Mostly, he stayed inside his shell.

Every day I told him stories—like how Dasha
got new overalls, and how Ruth lost a tooth,
and how Peter from downstairs got a fish.

I even told him my best joke about the walrus
wearing pants. But he didn't seem to get it.

After a while, I kind of forgot about Alfie. He didn't do much.
Well, until the morning of my seventh birthday, when . . .

. . . he disappeared.

When I first saw Nia, I knew she was special.

She told me that I was six, and she was six too.
I had never been six before, but I was happy
we were six, together.

Her home tickled my toes, but she smelled
nice, so I was calm.

She had tons of friends.

Nia taught me to dance! I practiced wiggling inside my shell.
She gave me presents! I had never been given presents.

She made me laugh and laugh and laugh.

How could I make her as happy as she made me?
I had to think.

And think and think.

Nia was planning her seventh birthday.
She told me we were going to be seven, together.

I had to find her a present.

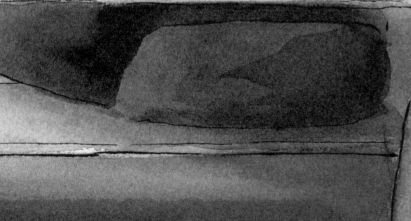

There were some good options behind the couch. But they were too dusty.

I looked in all the corners and shadows and cracks,

and found some great places,

but no great presents.

I asked Toby, and he said,

"YOU SHOULD TRY OUTSIDE!

OUTSIDE IS THE BEST!!

OUTSIDE IS THE BEST!!!

GET HER A STICK!"

I had never been outside before.

I climbed past stinky things and sweet things—
but nothing as fun as Nia.

I had to keep looking.

I had to take a risk.

I crunched through the reds and oranges and yellows,
but the longer I looked for a special one, the browner they got.

I found a nice blue cap, but it was too small for Nia's head.

There was nothing in the desert.

My toes were cold and my heart was sad.
I would never find a present as special as my friend.
The snail said all I needed was a good rest.

He knew the perfect place for me to take a nap.
"Just. Over. Those. Stones," he said.

So I napped.

And napped and napped.

When I woke up, I felt better. I asked the fish for help, and she showed me the things that had fallen to the bottom.

And then I saw it.

It was perfect.

It looked just like
something Nia would love.

I had to rush to the party.
When I finally got over the rocks,
the snail said, "That. Was. Fast."

I was right on time.

There she was.

I could tell Nia was very surprised and happy.
I had brought her the perfect present.

Now we were seven, together.

AUTHOR'S NOTE

On my sixth birthday, I got Alfie. In real life.

I loved everything about him at first. I made him food he didn't eat, and mazes he didn't run, and, well, I eventually lost interest. I lost interest for about twenty years. But then one evening, as an adult, I decided to follow Alfie around the house. I watched as he stuck his head in slippers and scratched his back on the radiator, and I became fascinated again. (The lucky thing about turtles is their lifespan is long enough for you to fall back in love with them.) I watched my little niece Nini become obsessed with Alfie, and the year after that I met my friend Nia, whose turtle, Max, is constantly escaping, and the story started to fall into place. This book is dedicated to Nini and Nia; to my wonderful agent, Stephen Barr, who's believed in this book from the beginning; and to my mom for taking such good care of Alfie all these years, even when I wasn't paying much attention.

The illustrations in this book were made with ink and watercolor.

Cataloging-in-Publication Data has been applied for
and may be obtained from the Library of Congress.

ISBN: 978-1-4197-2529-6

Text and illustrations copyright © 2017 Thyra Heder
Book design by Alyssa Nassner

Published in 2017 by Abrams Books for Young Readers, an imprint of ABRAMS.

Printed and bound in China
10 9 8 7 6 5 4 3 2 1

Abrams Books for Young Readers are available at special discounts when purchased in quantity for premiums and promotions as well as fundraising or educational use. Special editions can also be created to specification. For details, contact specialsales@abramsbooks.com or the address below.

ABRAMS The Art of Books
115 West 18th Street, New York, NY 10011
abramsbooks.com